THE ANTS AND THE GRASSHOPPER

NARRATED BY THE FANCIFUL BUT TRUTHFUL GRASSHOPPER

BY NANCY LOEWEN

ILLUSTRATED BY CARLES ARBAT

raintree

a Capstone company — publishers for children

Raintree is an imprint of Capstone Global Library Limited,
a company incorporated in England and Wales having its registered
office at 264 Banbury Road, Oxford, OX2 7DY – Registered company
number: 6695582

www.raintree.co.uk
myorders@raintree.co.uk

Edited by Jill Kalz
Designed by Lori Bye
The illustrations in this book were created digitally.
Original illustrations © Capstone Global Library Limited 2019
Production by Kris Wilfahrt
Originated by Capstone Global Library Ltd
Printed and bound in India

ISBN 978 1 4747 6208 3
22 21 20 19 18
10 9 8 7 6 5 4 3 2 1

British Library Cataloguing in Publication Data
A full catalogue record for this book is available from the British Library.

Acknowledgements
Design Element: Shutterstock, Audrey_Kuzman

A fable is a short animal tale that teaches a lesson. It is one of the oldest story forms. "The Ants and the Grasshopper" is from a collection of hundreds of fables called *Aesop's Fables*. These stories may have been written by Aesop, a Greek storyteller who lived from 620 to 560 BC.

In autumn, the ants were busy drying out the grain they had gathered in the summer. A hungry grasshopper came to them and asked for something to eat.

"Haven't you been storing food for the winter?" the ants asked. "What have you been doing all summer?"

The grasshopper held out a fiddle and said, "I've been making music. And before I knew it, summer was over!"

The ants shooed the grasshopper away. They didn't offer any food. "You've made your choice," they said. "Now live with it!"

The moral of the story:

There's a time for work and a time for play.

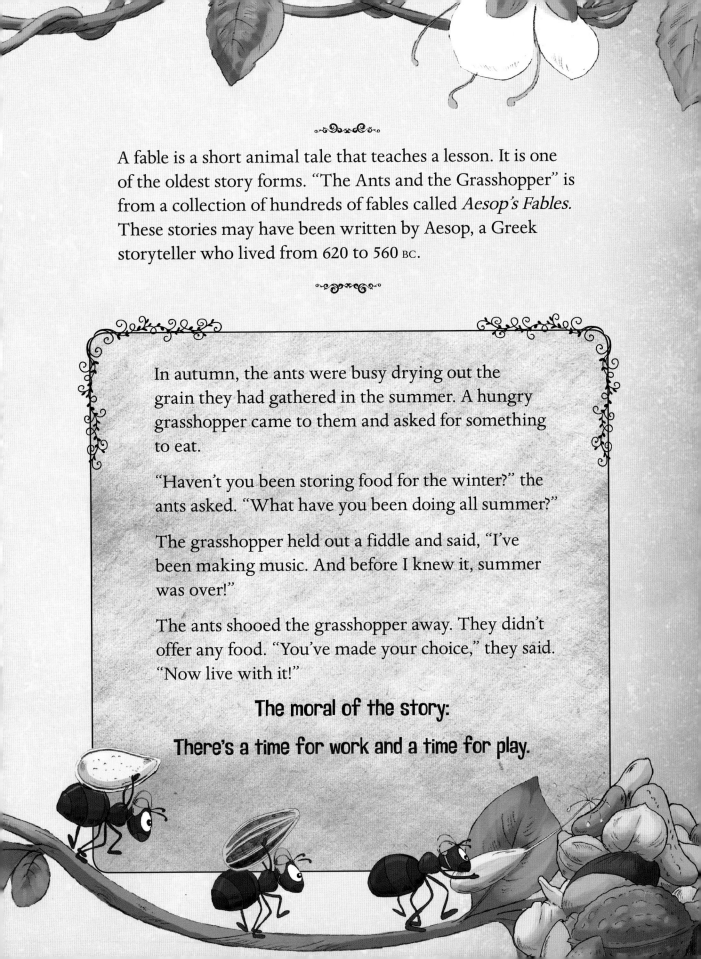

Oh, hello! I'm pleased to meet you. My name is Harper. I'm the grasshopper in the fable you've just read.

I want you to know that I am *not* lazy. Did I make some mistakes? Yes, I did. But that fable finishes just when the *real* story begins. The *rest* of the story hits all the right notes!

That summer was especially delightful. I loved everything about it: the rosy sunrises, the fresh grass, the blooming flowers, the gentle breezes . . . I felt so happy. I just *had* to play my fiddle. I *had* to sing.

I played my fiddle on the rainy days too.
That's when we need music the most.

The animals and insects in the meadow enjoyed my music very much. Not the ants, though. They barely looked up when I sang for them. As they busily dug tunnels and gathered seeds, they seemed to be marching to a beat of WORK-WORK-WORK.

I got so carried away with my music that I didn't notice the earlier sunsets or the fading flowers. The wind turned chilly. Leaves dropped from the trees.

Then one day, my stomach rumbled quite loudly. I looked around for a tender plant or seed to eat and found . . . nothing.

"Excuse me, could you spare a sunflower seed for a hungry musician?" I asked the ants.

"No, we could not!" one of them snapped.

"We worked hard all summer for our food," another said. "What did you do?"

Sadly, I turned away. Why hadn't I prepared for winter? What had I been thinking? I couldn't live without food. Soon the snow would fall, and that would be the end of me.

The day came when I was too weak to play my fiddle.

I thought I was dreaming when I heard a voice say, "Here, eat this." But then a kernel of wheat appeared before me. I bit into it. This was no dream. This was real! I took a few more bites and looked around to see who had been so kind.

"Hello," said a little ant, shyly. "My name is Lark. I really like your music."

"Thank you," I said. I hungrily finished off the kernel. Immediately, Lark gave me another one.

"You've saved my life," I told her. "How can I ever repay you?"

Lark looked down at her feet. She spoke softly. "Well, I was hoping – perhaps you could – teach me how to play the fiddle?"

"Really?" I asked in surprise. "But you're an ant. I thought ants didn't like music."

"This one does," Lark said. "Please, will you teach me? I'll pay you with food."

"Of course," I said. I was feeling stronger already. "It would be my pleasure."

Lark and I made a tiny new fiddle out of caterpillar silk
and a hollowed-out apple seed. We created a bow out of a
strip of reed. Then we got started with our lessons.

Lark learned quickly. In no time at all we were playing
beautiful songs together.

One day during practice, I noticed a couple of ants watching us. They were waving their feelers in time to the music.

Then I saw ladybirds swaying back and forth . . . and all sorts of other flying insects doing loops and spins in the air.

That's when I got an idea. I whispered it to Lark, and she nodded.

"Friends!" I called out. "Would you like to become musicians too?"

"I would!" shouted a ladybird.

"Me too!" called an ant.

"Count us in!" said a couple of dragonflies.

"All right, then," I said. "Let's make our very own orchestra!"

We got to work making our instruments.

I gave lessons day and night. Everyone paid me with food.
Soon I had more seeds than I knew what to do with!

Next we practised as a group. At first we sounded more like
out-of-tune crickets than a real orchestra. But we got better.

In fact, we got *so* good that we put on the first-ever Harvest Festival Concert. It was a smashing success!

So, is there a time for work and a time for play? Absolutely. But remember: *Make time for music and sharing too!*

THINK ABOUT IT

How would the story change if it was told from Lark's point of view? Or from the point of view of the other ants?

Describe how the character of Harper is different from the grasshopper in the original fable.

Should the ants have helped Harper when she asked for food? Why or why not?

Describe a time when you were paying such close attention to something that you lost track of what was going on around you.

GLOSSARY

Aesop Greek storyteller (620–560 BC) whose fables teach a lesson

character person, animal or creature in a story

fable short animal tale that teaches a lesson

instrument something used to make music

kernel seed and hard husk of a cereal, especially wheat

moral lesson about what is right and wrong

musician someone who plays music

orchestra large group of musicians who perform together, usually including string, wind and percussion instruments

point of view way of looking at something

READ MORE

The Frog Prince Saves Sleeping Beauty (Fairy Tale Mix-Ups), Charlotte Guillain (Raintree, 2016)

Illustrated Stories from Aesop, Susanna Davidson (Usborne Publishing, 2013)

Orchard Aesop's Fables, Michael Morpurgo (Orchard Books, 2014)

Why the Spider Has Long Legs (Folk Tales From Around the World), Charlotte Guillain (Raintree, 2014)

WEBSITES

www.bbc.co.uk/programmes/b03g64r9
Listen to some more stories from Aesop's Fables.

www.bbc.co.uk/guides/z24rxfr
Find out more about different types of stories.

LOOK FOR ALL THE BOOKS IN THE SERIES:

 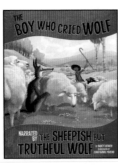